Jayant Bhagat

Evincepub
Publishing

Evincepub Publishing

Mansarover Park, West Delhi, India 110015
SMIG - 65, Parijat Extension, Bilaspur, Chhattisgarh 495001

First Published by Evincepub Publishing 2017
Copyright © Jayant Bhagat 2017
All Rights Reserved.
ISBN: 978-1-5457-1052-4

Then I met you

By

Jayant Bhagat

Disclaimer

This is a work of fiction. Names, characters, businesses, places, events and incidents are either the products of the author's imagination or used in a fictitious manner. Any resemblance to actual persons, living or dead, or actual events is purely coincidental.

Cigarette and Bidi both are Injurious to health.

Acknowledgement

I would like to express my gratitude to many people who helped me through this book.

I want to thank the four pillars of my life, my father, my mother, my brother and my friends, especially mentioning Satyarth Mani, Amit Gupta, Abhishek Maurya, Karun Mishra, Dileep Singh Gautam. They all supported me and encouraged even though it took me away from them.

I also take this opportunity to thank all the teachers of HOLY CROSS SCHOOL BALLIA who taught how to read and write, because without them I would not have been what I am today.

Thank you all, I am blessed that I got people like you in my life.

Prologue

All my life since my birth, I have been told by everyone that I needed to become something. I need to be professional in order to progress in life. I kept fighting with the world and myself just to become something until I met you.

I was having a great family, great friends and life was complete until you came and filled the blank not visible to me also.

I may have made thousands of mistakes, I may have not lived up to the expectations of my family and friends. I may have made many people happy and sad on the course of my journey. Someone of them might have blessed me some would have cursed me, I thank them all because they all led me up to you.

I was blessed with the fortunes of time, it has always shown me good things. But I never knew that it has reserved the best within itself until I met you.

I never planned to fall for you and I doubt the same for you. But once we met it was clear neither of us wanted to control what was happening to us.

This is not just a story, maybe it is not even love, but it is much more than that. Because it is about you.

And now since I met you I know that I do not need to become anything else but be myself…!

Dedication

Dedicated to: "You!"

Then I met you

"If You Promise To Remember Me Forever Then I Don't Care If Everbody Else Forgets"

Content Table

The best thing in life happens unexpectedly.

The best stories begin with the most unexpected person.

The best thing happens at the most unexpected time.

So free yourself from all expectations and let the most beautiful thing happen to you when you least expect.

Chapter 1

Mumbai

It all started with a Mumbai trip, which both of us were chosen by the organization for a pilot project. Pilot you guessed it right one who drives the plane, one who has the responsibility for the safety of the passengers. But imagine what will happen to the plane, which is driven by inexperienced pilots.

We had to leave for Mumbai from Delhi by train for a pilot project, I never understood why they called us pilots when we had to go by train. Anyhow, this is not about train, bus and plane but about a known stranger Aarushi.

We had to leave from Delhi to Mumbai and we were in the same coach on our middle berth's. Aarushi was upset for unknown reasons to me and talking to her friend shouting and yelling and crying at the same time.

I was a mere spectator at that time watching her doing all these. The train left at the right time against the laws of railways and she was busy doing her crying work.

I would like to mention about a person who was with us and was chosen for the same project, a dear friend of mine Avinash. Me and Avinash were not strangers but great collague's. He was senior to me in experience and my mentor also. We both were sitting together and gossiping about company as done by all the employees of an organization. Cursing the manager, the formats and field work, salary etc. Because all the employees and particularly the sales team believe that the entire company is dependent on them and if they fail to deliver than the organization will collapse. But anyhow, this conversation was the part of the daily routine between me and Avinash, it had nothing to do with reality just that it helps to release the mental pressure generated by our Managers.

We heard a voice "Tm log khana kha liye?" (You both had your food) from Aarushi. The eyes all red and totally in a depressed voice she asked.

We both were quite happy and excited about the project and yes, we had our dinner, we hardly cared about her stuff and carelessly replied together in the same note,

"Ha kyu tm nahi kha ke aye ho kya?" (yes we had, did not you).

And continued the ongoing conversation which we believed was more important than the hunger of the crying lady. She interrupted in between again and said,

"Yar mai to tm log ke sath dinner karna chahti thi" (I wanted to have dinner with you all).

"Madam we did not dream about your thoughts, you must have told us before", Avinash replied to her in a little sarcastic tone.

"Now you will get only biscuits to eat because the pantry will start only in the morning", I said trying to stop all the conversation at once which I thought could turn into an argument and spoil the entire journey and the training period.

We arranged snacks for her and Avinash went on to sleep on the top berth. Me and Aarushi on the middle berths lying upside down, she was busy talking to her friend and me in my song collection. Me and Aarushi belong to the same city, same school, same college, same company but had never known each other or talked to each other all these years, although faced almost every day. We knew each other, but still were strangers.

We arranged snacks for her and Avinash went on to sleep on the top berth. Me and Aarushi on the middle berths lying upside down, she got busy talking to her friend after the dinner cum supper with the snacks and me went on with my song collection, after about half an hour when she had almost finished her yelling and I decided to take a little break I asked her gently,

"Are you ok?"

It was my nature never to initiate the conversation and also I had a negative perception of her, that she is too arrogant so I never bothered to talk to her. However the crying lady fetched my attention and all those perceptions were kept aside. I mean, who will leave an opportunity to talk to the girl and that also as pretty as Aarushi when you know that the next 7 days you have to be with her. The conversation did not have any relevance because we were just strangers who knew each other and yet it went for long hours just whispering to each other so that it do not disturb the other passengers. I don't know at what time did whisper stopped and we went to sleep.

Morning, I got up because of the useless hue and cry that the fellow passengers created. I did not understand it because at night I took utmost care so that they don't get disturbed and now they are careless about my sleep.

Anyhow, what can I do for it and jumped out of my place to see that Aarushi is eating her food from pantry and was enjoying like hell. I saw that her eating process has grabbed the attention of almost everyone to whom she was visible but she hardly cared.

"I guess that was the reason she was crying and yelling last night." I said to Avinash as he handed me the cup of tea.

I learned a lesson, a hungry women is as dangerous as your boss, shouting for known reasons.

The train reached the MUMBAI CENTRAL railway station and we got off took our cab to the hotel RAMADA.

———— ◆ ————

Chapter 2

Juhu Beach

B.E.A.C.H

The Best Escape Anyone Can Have

The next day after the training from 9:30 to 5:00 pm, we had planned to go the famous Juhu beach because it is where we can escape from the horrible company of our managers. Me and Avinash decided to go there and got ready. Aarushi had to do whatever me and Avinash would decide because she didn't have many options to try.

The Juhu beach in Mumbai is one of the most famous Indian beaches. It boarders one of the most posh locality where most of the celebrities stay and therefore the probability of finding them walking and jogging is very high. Also, it has one of the most famous street food centers, which marks the legacy of the financial capital of India. All this with added natural beauty and peaceful atmosphere can excite anyone to visit the place.

We reached the beach and it was an amazing full of people and things around, looked like a happening place. Me and Avinash already had visited to this place, still were excited about it. We were just roaming at the edge as water come and leave our footsteps. It is an amazing feeling when you walk on the shore like this, not only because of the water but also the cold breeze and lovely faces. You don't need anybody's company to walk along the Juhu beach because the environment itself is a great companion over there. So me and Avinash both were walking along in our own thoughts and Aarushi was just following us.

Suddenly, I heard a screaming voice, "Jay, Jay", and turned to see the innocent creature sitting at one point holding her leg.

It was Aarushi, as careless as we were always "Kya hua?" we said together in the same tone with a smile.

"Something has beaten me on my leg please see" She replied.

We bend to see her and just ignored saying its just an insect Aarushi, nothing else and made her stand.

"Let's walk", I said, holding her hand and moving in one direction.

She hated when we did that because anybody on planet earth must have seen it more closely and at least tried to console a pretty lady as her but not we. She whispered again,

"Jay it is very painful and it is itching like anything" .

"What?" I bend to see.

I asked Avinash to light up the phone torch so that we can see that. Her legs had turned red all around her ankle and then we realized this is something else. I just held her hand and started to walk to the distant light area so that we can make a conclusion out of it. She held my hand with a tight grip which marked the pain she was going through.

I have nothing to explain about that moment what that felt to walk 200 m with holding her hand, looking at her so closely and with an expectation of what could go wrong if something happens to her. All the pros and cons started to occupy my thoughts, "what will I answer to the people if something happens to her, what if this is the bite of a snake? What if she die? No no cant be so I said to myself as we reached a shop. I washed her legs as many times possible and just console her that nothing will happen, but to be very frank we were very frightened as well. Her face had turned red which added to the beauty which she had naturally, but at this point of time I did not have courage to mention her all this.

"It will be fine Aarushi", Avinash said, trying to console her and reducing the tension which was clearly visible on our faces. I did not have anything to say because I was really worried from inside, but I have to be manly also and didn't have to show my emotions to any girl, so I went on to take a cigarette, as done by all the smokers in a tensed situation. I light it up and came to them standing in one place and all the three of us were in silent mode for next few minutes. Avinash was facing the shore and was in a deep thought mode and me and Aarushi were facing each other with me standing in front of her and looking deep into her eyes, we kept staring into each other's eyes without a blink.

Nothing to say about Aarushi, she looked so pretty with a natural glimpse of innocence on her face and with her brown eyes and a black spot in her left eye.

Our staring process went on for a minute or two before I realized that half of my cigarette has been wasted looking at her, but anyhow, I was smoking just to reduce the tension in my mind and that was done by looking at her so it was not a waste of 12 bucks, which I spent for the cancer causing agent. I took two long puffs of my stuff and blew it in the air and threw it with a style on the ground.

"Koch khila do bhukh lagi hai" (I am hungry please buy me something to eat) is what I and Avinash heard in a sweet and low pitch voice.

Me and Avinash looked at each other and then laughed for next few seconds Aarushi joined in the laughter a little later, and we both hugged her.

"Tujhe kuch nahi hone denge" we said in the same voice and note to her. The girl, who was a stranger to both of us, suddenly with one incident came so close that we could actually hug her. However, the realization of the fact that she is fine now was more important than the hug.

We enjoyed the famous Pav Bhaji of Mumbai and she was eating like she did not have food from the last decade or so. Me and Avinash looked at her all these moments and we smiled, looking at each other, but did not bother to distract the innocent creature. We finished our eating and took auto for the hotel Ramada.

Chapter 3

Unknown Call

"When the past calls, let it go to the voicemail,

Believe me it has nothing new to say."

We reached the hotel around 9:45 and were headed towards our room before we hear again from Aarushi "Dinner kab kiya jayega?" (when will we have our dinner?)

"What?" me and Avinash said in the same note together.

"Janmo se bhukhe ho kya?" (are you hungry since ages) We said in the same note together again.

"Nahi yar yaha chicken bahut badhiya banta hai" (chicken is very famous) is what she replied, which made us laugh again.

Let's go I said   without asking any further question. we went on to the dinner area, because I already knew that if she won't eat then she will again yell and cry at night as she did last night in the train.

The dinner area of Ramada was a happening place at that time because the participants of the Indian Idol Junior were staying in that hotel and the parents of the kids were taking care of them. The kids were singing and running over here and there trying to avoid the food as done by most of them. They all sang sometimes in chorus and sometimes alone which had made the dining area a lively place. Otherwise, the well known corporate people have been gifted with a unique talent to ruin the atmosphere and make it stressful without reasons at all. We entered there and found a very corner seat for us. Avinash took some salads and me some soup for myself. Nothing to mention about the lady she was fond of chicken so she took all the time finding the right pieces and all the food items and came after 10 minutes. We were discussing about the things that we learned today in our training session. She kept herself busy with her food and hardly cared about the discussion we were going through.

"Abe yar ye kaha se aa gaye!" (from where did they came), she said breaking our conversation.

we turned together to see the 2 managers entering the dinner area.

"Aur kha lo", Is what me and Avinash replied again in the same tone angrily.

"Whenever she opens her mouth something goes wrong this is what I was observing last few hours", I said in a prompt voice.

"So guys enjoying", asked by one of them as they reached our table.

"Abhi tak to tha age ka pata nahi" (till now we were but don't have an idea about the next) she whispered, which was audible to both of them.

They did not find anything to answer her, but still took the chair beside us. As I mentioned about the unique talent of corporate people they started.

This is very great opportunity for all the 3 of you, you have been chosen because of your performance on all India basis, make sure you learn and use this opportunity for your growth in the organization and all the motivational stuffs told by one of them.

"Sir kuch assignments mile hai, agar aap bura na mane to hum log jaye wo finish karne hai" (we have to finish our assignments if you allow can we go?) Avinash said at one pace.

"Yeah yeah please go ahead" they both replied together and we did not bother to wash our hands .

We all replied together "Thank you sir, and good night", and walked out as we have escaped death. Took the stairs and reached our room.

We all sat together in the room and started to do the assignments, helping each other learn the things that was taught today. Just to mention here that the training was mainly for introduction of iPads a masterpiece from Apple in our daily field work. We were working as a Medical Representative in one of the top MNC in India and we use visual aids for discussing our products to the doctors. The company has now planned to introduce iPds in place of visual aids for the field force. We did all the learning process in less than an hour as we are technology driven generation guys.

"It looked hard in the training, but in fact it is very easy", Aarushi completed her sentence and her phone rang.

"Who the hells calls you at this time at night" I said and took the phone to see it, "Babu" I said who the hell is Babu I said and laughed.

"Are madam ka boyfriend hoga".(madam's boyfriend) Avinash said.

She did not reply to us and left the room. We did not even cared about her reply. Let's go to sleep, I said and light my cigarette. Avinash asked me to close all the lights. I went into my bed just to lie down because I was hardly feeling anything but sleep. I never had this feeling of restlessness inside me because I was too busy with my stuffs, but today I was a bit uncomfortable, I did not know the reason so I was trying to figure it out. I started to recapitulate the entire day's events and everthing looked fine ,everything was perfect except Babu. Patted my head, no it can't be so, I said to myself, what the hell I have to do with Aarushi even if she has a boyfriend. I never had been in contact and I can't like her. She is not the girl I ever thought of even in the wildest of my dreams, even though I faced her almost every day.

.   "No No!" it can't be so. I just shrugged all the thoughts of it and hide myself inside the pillow trying to sleep.

After a while a voice of door opening went through my ears with a little light's of corridor, taking away the darkness of the room. A structure entering inside with a whisper said "Jay! Avinash! So gaye kya tm log yar?" (Have you guys slept?).

"Hum log nishachar nahi hai!" (We are not nocturnal) is what me and Avinash replied together in the same tone.

"How can both of you speak the same words and same note", Aarushi asked in a confused voice.

I switched on the light and me and Avinash busted out in laughter. Make some tea for us I said in a sarcastic tone and lighted one more cigarette and started to smoke.

"Boyfriend hai tmhara?"(is he your boyfriend) Avinash asked the question which was popping in my head.

"Yes", she said, and started to make the tea. There was a few minutes of silence before the tea was ready.

"Here it is", she said and handed over the mug to both of us, hope you guys like it.

"This is a machine made tea madam, there is no such talent of yours in its just you have poured everything in the hot water and gave it to us", Avinash said and looked at me.

"Yeah, it is right!" I said.

"But anyhow you have poured the stuffs in the right amount and that show you are talented", I said and smiled in order to cover for the sarcasm of Avinash. Everyone went into a deep thought for some time.

"Whenever you guys want to sleep, please let me know I will go to my room", Aarushi said and looked at me.

"I need some fresh air, Avinash, you want to come", I asked getting up from the bed.

"I need sleep", he replied.

"Can I come", asked the lady.

"I won't bother you."

"There is nothing to bother, you have your own legs you have to walk on your own", I replied.

I took my cigarette and went out of the room, closing the light behind and Aarushi followed me. I was like willing to ask her about "Babu" but did not. After a few minutes Aarushi said, have I done some mistake that you guys have your mood off.

"What makes you think that", I replied.

"Before the phone call you guys were cheering and now", she said.

"No, nothing like that, just that we are tired that's all", I replied to her.

Me and Aarushi have been together for such a long time facing each other daily so an unknown bonding was always there, just that we had never spoken to each other which we were doing now. So sharing her personal stuffs was not a very tough task to her, I was not a stranger or I may say a known stranger.

"His name is Abhishek and we are in relation from past 14 years", she said and continued

"I have already talked to my parents and we are getting married next year".It took some time to digest that and I stopped her and said

"What?"

"How old are you?" was my first question.

"25", she replied.

"You mean to say you are in a relation since age 11, are you kidding me, how can anybody understand all those stuffs at the age 11. We even did know what Pythagoras Theorem was at that age, and you choose your life partner at the same, that can't be true man means that is child marriage against the laws of the constitution, how can anyone do that?" I said all in one breathe.

To which she replied "What is Pythagoras theorem? I still don't know".

I laughed seeing the ignorance of the pretty lady.

"Be my friend" she said in a soft voice, there are a lot of people who have pretended to be my friends (she was talking about boys, girls hardly do friendship is what I concluded from her words) they all wanted one single thing. I have no friends to talk and share about me, you are very nice person I know, please be my friend".

"I am not your friend Aarushi, we are just on a business trip lets enjoy our training and get back to our work. I will make sure you don't find any problem on this trip and will make you reach Delhi safe that's my promise. I closed all the conversation at once and started to walk back to my room leaving her alone in the corridor at one place, which was very ruthless and reasons for such behavior was even unknown to me. I am closing the doors from inside meet you in the morning, good night I shouted from a my room and she just waved back.

Chapter 4

Pin Drop Silence

"Silence is the best way to tell some that you did wrong.

Silence is the most powerfull scream."

Next morning, we got up and dressed and decided to go to Aarushi's room on the 5th floor to take her for the meeting. Avinash rang the bell and the door opened in just a second. Aarushi was wearing a nice pink suit and combing her hair.

"Bas 2 minutes" she said and went on with the combing process. We went inside just to see that all her bed was covered with clothes scattered.

"iPads charge kiya hai madam?" (Did you charge your iPads?) Avinash asked.

"Are yar nahi, ab"(I did not what now?) she said.

"Kuch nahi chalo kuch solution nikala jayega aur kya"(we will find some solution) avinash replied.

She completed her dressing and we went to the dinning area for the breakfast, just to see both our managers having their breakfast together. We wished them "Good morning sir!"

"Be quick guys it is 8:40 we have to reach by 9:00.", one of them said.

"Sir lunch thodi karna hai? 10 min me ho jayega" (we don't have to do lunch, it will hardly take 10 minutes) I said with a sarcastic smile and went to take the juice and some fruit in my plate. We completed the breakfast in just 10 minutes and went to the assembly hall for the training. That day, there was arrangement for all the teams to sit together and we were representing the Delhi team.

"Aaj band bajne wali hai", (it will be a horrible today) Avinash whispered in my ears.

"Aaj ye dono hamare sath rahenge on the same table" (both the managers will be sitting on the same table with us together). We sat on the table, all the five of us.

The meeting started and went on for about an hour before the first tea break. Me and Avinash were busy in understanding all the stuffs and hardly looked at Aarushi what she was doing. She was trying to make an eye contact with both of us, but we hardly cared. After the tea break there was a recapitulation session and one member from each team had to present it. The managers have to choose that member and what they choose off course Aarushi, ladies first said one of them with a big laugh on his face and horrible yellow teeth. Aarushi went to the center and started to narrate the learning just to find herself in a confused state only after 3-4 sentences. She stood there for about a minute without uttering a word and said sorry only to come back to her seat.

"It's ok, you will learn it as you practice" said the training manager.

But this event busted both the managers as they thought it has spoiled the reputation of the Delhi team. They both started to scream at her in the next tea break and scolded both of us asking all the useless stuffs and degrading our confidence. Me and Avinash were very confident because we thought we have learned all the stuffs very nicely and this useless scolding we are getting because of this pretty lady. But anyhow managers need to find something in their subordinates that is what they are paid for.

"You all are champions behave like that", was the last sentence they both said. I was totally out of my mind and needed to break the monotony, so I did what I always do, went to smoke and came back for the meeting. Aarushi was not uttering a single word from her mouth and also was not looking at us after the tea break. She was busy learning or I can say busy in avoiding managers shit. We broke for lunch and 3 of us went together to the place where the lunch was served.

The best part of corporate meetings is the food that we get. They are beautifully decorated and garnished and always prompting. It had all the non veg items like lobster and chicken, fish almost everthing. Almost all the veg items that as middle class grown up I can think off.

"I will try something new, which I don't eat regularly", a thought crossed my mind.

I went on to take some lobster and saw that Aarushi was just eating salad.

"Chicken bhi hai" I said (chicken is available).

"To kya kare nahi khana hai, hum kuch bhi khaye tmse matlab" (so what should I do, I don't need your suggestion for the food) she said angrily.

"Ok just relax dude why are you angry, it is not my fault that you could not answer and by the way it is perfect you need not to answer everytime a question is asked to you", I said adding some intellect in my words. She did not reply to me or I may say she did not have words for that intellectual answer.

Avinash came in between and he did not know what the conversation was and politely said "Are madam aap chicken nahi kha rahe badhiya bana hai" (madam you are not having chicken it is very delicious) and I busted out in laughter just to get everybody's attention and a horrible stare from a giant creature my immediate manager.

"Tum log dono sale ek jaise ho" she said (you both are alike) and went to bring the delicious chicken in her plate.

"Happy both of you, you go and smoke lunch time is about to get over", she said.

"Wow! thanks for making me remember that I need to smoke." "You will burn your lungs, Jay why don't you understand."

"So what! Are we going to get married if I don't smoke? I am not going to be your husband so stop pretending like my wife or girlfriend", I replied to her and left.

The meeting was resumed and again the recapitulation session started and again Aarushi was asked to represent the team, but contrary to earlier performance she did a fantastic job this time and was highly applauded for her effort.

"Food is the main problem creator, look at her how she explained everthing after the lunch", I whispered to avinash.

"Abe chhod na tujhe kya karna hai, just clap". (Leave it what you have to do for it). He said.

We joined the audience and clapped and that also with a high note not because she did well, but because I and Avinash thought it is a great exercise as it increases the blood flow in the hands and reduces the dizziness that we were feeling after the lunch. Anyhow the day finally came to an end and we packed all our stuff and went back to our rooms. Aarushi did not come to our room today and we also did not bother to call her. Me and Avinash decided to go for a walk and see the Hiranandani building which was near to our hotel. We went there and both of us were astonished to see the beautiful building and the shopping malls all around. There were pretty faces, we both live in Delhi and had a very good experience with the beauty and the swag the Delhi girls carry.

"But yaha log bahut jayda open hai, apne layak nahi hai" (girls are very modern here not of our class)Avinash said, looking at a girl who just parked her Mercedes and came out wearing hipster and a sleeveless and goggles on her eyes. She just went to a nearby cigarette shop and light one up and started to smoke puffing in the air and making circles of the smoke. Looking at this I threw the small cigarette and went with my swag to light a new one, just to see a Range Rover entered the parking area. A giant muscular spectacular may be bachelor as well came out of it and walked to the same shopand before I could figure out hugged the same girl.

"Iski ...", (what the f***).

All the swag that I was carrying went down and I went back to sit beside Avinash.

"Bhai mal chahiye to paisa kamana padega" he said (if you want girlfriend, you need to earn)

"Sahi bat hai" (that's true) I replied and got up.

"Let's go to the hotel", I said.

It was 8:30 at night and we decided that we will have our dinner now as I was feeling hungry. We went into the dining area, and saw Aarushi and both the managers were having dinner together. We just ran from the place competing to reach the finishing line to our room and made sure no one notices. After about an hour the door bell rang and I opened just to see Aarushi standing at the door, we have to do our assignments together is what, sir has said, before I could reply her she came in and took the most distant chair and started her work.

"We have to have our dinner before we do all this. Let's go Avinash!", I said and started to walk.

"Wait, wait, what's your problem Jay? Why are you being so rude to me?"

"What the hell I did now?" I said.

"Why the hell you both did not take me with you in the evening".

"Because of both of you I had to spend my evening with these 2 idiots," she said, and tears rolled down her cheek, her eyes turning red and she started with a stammering voice,

"What is that I have done wrong that both of you are behaving in such a rude manner, you owe me an answer".

"Nothing you have done nothing just that we thought that if you wanted to go you must have come to the room, but you did not and we went that's all".

"Don't cry "Khana to kha chuke ho ab kyu ro rahe ho", (don't cry you already had your food) Avinash said just to make her smile.

"Don't complicate Aarushi and don't expect just enjoy the things and get back to work" I said and we went to have our dinner and came back just to complete our assignments. We did it all together and at around 11 the phone rang. Aarushi took the phone went out without uttering a single word and we did not ask any question as well.

"I am going to sleep", Avinash said. I need a walk so I took my packet of cigarette went to the lawn and walked all around with a pin drop of silence, although it was horrible in my head, popping a lot of unwanted questions, useless answers and uneasiness inside the heart. I light the second cigarette and carried out my walking process just to see Aarushi heading towards the lawn.

"It is a kind of routine work for you talking to him at the same time and I think the same question everyday", I asked as soon as she reaches close to me.

She gazed at me without answering and I did not find anything to say after that. We walked together side by side for about half an hour with Pin Drop Silence before I said

"Lets go to sleep it is very late".

We went to our respective rooms without even wishing each other as I thought night won't be good for both of us. There was a series of emotions I was going through and still I did not know what were they. By nature I am happy and optimistic person. I have always been looking at the brighter side of any one I meet. I usually believe that world is full of brightness, love and possibilities to seize. However, my behavior towards Aarushi was rude and the reasons were unknown to me. I never had spent time with her before so how can I behave that way and what she must be thinking about me about all these gestures. I don't know what is happening to me and I don't know why is happening ?

Chapter 5

Cocktail

"You can't buy happiness but you can buy wine they are almost one and the same thing"

Next day the same routine was followed, but it was different Aarushi today. She was dressed in black, formal suit and lots of Kajal in her eyes and a ponytail of hairs on her face, which surpasses her eyes and reaches the neck, she always had to push them back on her ears in order to get a clear view. But all these decorations added to the pretty face and makes me more prompting to her. I could not resist myself of complementing her, you are looking awesome, I whispered in her ears as we all 5 together sat on the table before the training session began. Thank you she said with a gentle smile as we stared each other for a few seconds and I gave her the thumbs up sign.

"So today will be a very exciting day for the field force because you will be given the opportunity to monitor your managers of what they have learned till now", said the training manager and it made the entire hall laugh at once.

"Yes, these managers have always judged you and give you feedback about your work so we thought we should give at least one chance to monitor the Hippocrates", and the hall busted out in laughter once again. The session began and managers were given different assignments to do and we were sitting ideally just observing them. We realized in the process that these guys are very poor with their handling process of this technically genius gadget and the company has done a mistake by handing over this I pads a masterpiece of Steve Jobs.

"Anyhow, what we have to do with it, let the fellows be busy in this so that they won't wear out our head", Avinash whispered in my ears.

The day went out this way and since free wifi was available me and Avinash updated all our applications and downloaded Templerun on our iPads and played all day just competing and beating each other.

The day ended with an announcement that today we will all be having a cocktail party to celebrate this new specification in our field work. We were more than happy as me and Avinash both love to drink, but Aarushi said

"What is this and what for the people who don't drink".

"There will be juices madam", me and Avinash said together in the same tone with a sarcastic smile.

"Very funny", she replied and we went to our respective rooms.

At around 7:00 the doorbell rang, I opened the door to see a lady with a beautiful black dress which ended just over the knees with a high heel sandal and her back facing the door.

"Yes please", I said and the lady turned to face me.

"Aarushi, I took a long breath, Aarushi wow man you look just like Kareena Kapoor", was what I said, not to mention that Kareena Kapoor was my favourite actress in the film industry.

"Really well, thank you let me come in", and she walked to sit on her favourite chair.

"Avinash, it is 7 and you both are still not ready."

"Ab kya ready hona hai, ab to sare party me tm law of gravity ki tarah kam karogi, koi kisi ko nahi dekhega" (why to get ready now everyone will only stare at you in the party), Avinash replied to her and popped out of his bed.

"I need a favor, although you are looking exceptionally pretty, but if you can please cook some tea, it will be very nice", I asked her.

She busted out in laughter.

"Cook nahi make hota gadha(donkey)" (it is not cook but make donkey) and Avinash laughed with her and I was alone with a gentle smile. I did not understand why food is cooked and tea is made. But any how her laughter on my ignorance was great to see.

"Whatever please do it and I will get ready".

We all got ready in 10 minutes and went to the party. It already had begun and the managers were present, Aarushi got everybody's attention as expected and we both poor fellows went with our work. After 2-3 drinks both the managers called me and Avinash to a corner place.

"Are you guys ok", asked one of them.

"Sir abhi to start kiya hai" (sir we have just started) we replied together in the same tone and a smile.

"We have got a lot of complaint regarding both of you, kindly behave properly or we have to take some serious action.", The man with the fat face said.

"What??" we both again said together.

"What complain you are talking about sir, what have we done" I asked.

All the dizziness of the alcohol has just vanished and we were in full control of our senses now. The people from the other team have complained that Aarushi stays in your room for very long at night, and also they have found you (pointing towards me) walking with her late night on the lawn.

"So what? You only have said that learn together and we do our assignments in our room that's it".

"But you all are not allowed to have her in your room with close doors."

"What?" I shouted

"Have you totally lost your mind or what?" I said angrily.

"How can anyone say like this, we are on the same team and we have to complete our assignments together as instructed by you, and what the hell the door has to do with all this, I think you have totally lost your mind boss "I said with a loud voice and angry tone to get every bodies attention.

"Control yourself Jay! This was said by people and we just wanted both of you to know about the image people have started to make of you all three. Shear amount of silence for a few minutes, you both guys are champions and you should understand that people will find opportunity to find faults in you and you both should therefore not be casual at any cost in your behavior.

"To hell with the champions and to hell with the team, why you both haven't defended us", Avinash shouted."

I think alcohol have started to do its work, we were fearless. Otherwise, who can talk to their bosses like this, I thought to myself. Let me join Avinash.

"Why did you not say that it was your instruction to complete the assignments together. I said and went to take a drink.

"Avinash behave properly or you both can get punished for this. The company is very strict when it comes to integrity of women employees."

"Sir, we are just doing our training and the exercise as instructed by you and nothing else, if you can trust us, that's well and good if you don't, it is not my problem", I said and completed my drink.

"Come on Avinash lets go."

We left the party and went to a near wine shop.

"They all are jealous, they have not seen a pretty lady and that is why they are pointing all this, idiots". I said and went on to have 3-4 vodka shots before the phone rang. I picked up the phone.

"Where are you I tried to search in all the possible places I could. Where are you? Please tell". Aarushi asked.

"Shadi karoge mujhse?" (will you marry me?) I replied.

"Kar lenge, agar tmhare reputation ko koi problem na ho to" (I will if it does not spoil your reputation) she said.

"Ab batao kaha ho, please" (now tell me where are you).

"We will come back in 15 minutes, just wait". I said, hanging the phone.

"What the hell was that?", Avinash asked.

"Why, what happened?" I replied.

"You proposed to Aarushi for marriage", Avinash said.

"Abe chad gaye hai tujhe" (you have lost your conscious) I replied. Just to make him feel that I did not know what I did. However, I myself was not clear as to why I did that and what made her reply positively.

"She must be drunk also", I said in my mind.

We finished our drinks and went back to the hotel. She was on her phone waiting outside the hotel. I looked at my watch and figured out who she must be talking to.

"We are going to the room come there only", Avinash said as we bypassed her.

We both were in our beds in a thoughtful mood and she came to sit over to the same chair. We did not utter anything and were deep in our thoughts.

"Is everything ok why you both are so silent today".

"Nothing you had your dinner, asked Avinash".

"Yes, what about you?"

"We had our drinks", he replied.

"I need some fresh air, anybody want to join?", asked Avinash.

"No", I said.

Aarushi pointed out her ankle just to show that she was tired. Avinash left for the walk and I took a comfortable position with my pillows behind my head.

"Please pass the ashtray", I asked Aarushi pointing to the distant table where the tray was lying. She passed the tray with her left hand and I grabbed her hand to pull her close to me. Just to see a nice ring in the middle finger of her left hand, I took the ring out of her middle finger and placed it on Ring Finger. Without saying anything, just held her hand for a few seconds, she did not react, but a drop of water droplet falls my hand. She started to cry and tears started to roll down her checks all of a sudden. I wiped away the tears and cleaned the Kajal in her eyes.

"This is much better", I said.

No words, no reply nothing just stare from her.

"Go back to your room", I said and pulled myself inside the sheet and closed all the light.

Chapter 6

The proposal

"All I wanted was someone to care for me
All I wanted was someone who was there
for me
All I wanted was someone who is true to
me

All I ever wanted was someone like you."

The next three days were as usual for the training and me and Avinash made sure that nothing unusual happened which give people an opportunity to question any one of us. So the same routine followed. Tomorrow will be the last day of our training so please all of you go through all the things that we have learnt and feel free to clear all your doubts before you leave tomorrow, said the training manager to conclude the day.

"Let's have some fun, I have never been on any training before this and it was a great experience with you both lets finish it off with a grand party", Aarushi said as we entered the corridor of the hotel.

"What party! You don't even drink and we do not have a party without it", Avinash said as I unlocked the room.

"A friend of mine, she lives in Mumbai has her birthday today and when I called her last night she has invited me for the celebration.

"Your friend so she must have invited you what the hell it has to do with us, If you want, you can go, we cannot go to an unknown party."

"Come on guys, it will be fun and anyhow you both will enjoy I promise, please!" Aarushi completed.

"Kyu bhai kya kehte ho?" (what do you say?), Avinash asked me.

"Daru hogi" I asked Aarushi.

"Yes" she said.

"Ok then we don't need anything else to enjoy", I said pointing to Avinash.

We got ready in an hour and she entered with a beautiful white dress.

I don't know how many dresses did she had and how everything suited her. We as boys have only trouser and shirt in formals and jeans and a t shirt as casual wear.

"Katil lag rahe ho". (looking gorgeous) Avinash said as soon as we saw her.

She did not reply anything, just looked at me as asking my opinion about it.

"Nice dress!" I said as I can read her mind and did not want to hurt her.

"Thank you". She said.

We booked a cab for Ghatkopar. The pint room was the address given to us by Aarushi. We reached there and the party had already gone on, loud music and smoke all over the bar. I was astonished by the atmosphere and concluded that the bars in the movies are not fake they really exist, all kinds of wine and different shades of clothing. The girls all dressed in the most fashionable clothes possible and loud music, which I like most.

"Bhai sab ki sab mal lag rahe hai" (every girl is pretty over here), Avinash said in my ears.

"Sabke boyfriends bhi hai" (everyone has a boyfriend as well) I replied with a smile.

"Yeah true, so what lets enjoy the atmosphere."

They all welcomed us as if we had been friends since our childhood. The overwhelming response from them made us very comfortable within no time and we started the procedure of drinks, first was vodka shorts which I took 5 at one time, however Avinash refused for it. It struck me like anything and I started to sing the songs that also in a loud voice, who cares man no one know me I thought to myself. They all loved it because I can sing any song played over there with the correct lyrics.

"It is my hobby to learn the lyrics of the songs", I said to them as they all were staring at me.

"Goodman that is great," said one the guy sitting over there.

"Thank you" I replied and started to have my drink. I did notice in between that Aarushi was looking at me continuously, but I tried to avoid her.

"Can you do me a favour?", I asked the buddy sitting beside me,

"Yes, why not" he said.

"Can I sing a song if possible",

"Yes, why not", he said and made all the arrangements for me to sing.

I dedicate this song on behalf of Raj to the birthday girl (they were both couples and were about to get married in a few months time), they all clapped and I started...

"Sari rat aahe bharta pal pal yado me marta,

mane na meri man mera,

thode thode hosh madhoshi se hai ,

neend behoshi se hai, jane ne kuch bhi na man mera."

(Song from the movie table no 21).

I kept staring at Aarushi eyes and completed the song, and was applauded by the entire genetry present over there. They all clapped and many of them hugged me, but I did not take my eyes away for a single moment from Aarushi and so did she. I went closer to her,

"Will you dance with me", I asked and she stood.

We went to the dance floor gently held each other staring into each others eyes for quite some time before she hugged me.

"I love you Jay, but I won't be able to marry you," she whispered in my ears and the clock ticked 11 and her phone rang. I gently pushed her aside and went to take some more shots before Raj came to me.

"You smoke, he asked me. That was like the best question anybody could ask me at that moment.

"Yes I do", and we both lit one cigarette.

The whisper of Aarushi words was still ringing in my ear. I was not sure as to what made her propose me and that also with hidden terms and condition. I have been listening to the love stories of my friends since my childhood, but I have never come across any story with a promise of love with a condition as ridiculous as that. Even God doesn't have the sense of understanding a women, looked so true to me.

"I will see to it", I said to myself and paused all the useless procastration my mind has started to create.

"I think we should leave now", I said.

"No, not all, at 12 we will cut the cake for her and then only you all will leave", raj replied to me pointing to the birthday girl.

We reached the hotel after completing all the party work and went to our respective rooms in silence. It was a well organized party, we had a lot of fun and the dizziness of alcohol added to it.

"Money can't buy happiness, but it can buy alcohol and I think they are one and the same thing."

Avinash said as he took his place in the bed.

The doorbell rang, "who is it?", Avinash shouted. No reply "who is it", he again asked reaching the door.

"It is me", a soft voice of Aarushi was audible to both of us.

"Can I come in if you guys are not sleeping", she asked and went to sit on her favourite chair before we could reply to her. I don't know why people ask when they don't care about the reply. However, it was not the time to fight. Every one of us knew that this is the last night of our training and once we reach Delhi we will hardly get time to meet each other.

Nobody was speaking anything and there was silence all around.

"It is all over now, again the same routine", Aarushi said breaking the monotony.

"So what did you thought?, that you will keep enjoying the training all your life and the company will keep paying for you". Avinash replied. She was used to such replies in the past seven days, so she hardly cared about this now.

We started to recapitulate all that has happened in the past week and enjoyed it. We were astonished to see how the things just in a span of 7 days have created a bondage between us. How Aarushi who was a stranger to me and Avinash has become a good friend. There were many things to take from this company sponsored trip, but still there were some unknown fear inside me and Aarushi which we could not discuss. I have not answered her for her proposal and her eyes were waiting for the answer. I was also in a confused state. Did not what to say and what not.

Anyhow, I never wanted this night to get over. I was going through an emotion which I have never felt before. I knew that I can gaze at her all my life without a blink, that was the bonding which I have developed for her in these 7 days. The person I avoided the most has got over me and I was figuring out as to how to move further in this relation. Avinash was half asleep and so was Aarushi in my bed. I closed all the lights and just went to my bed to sleep beside Aarushi, I made sure that ample amount of distance is maintained between me and her. I just kept my hand gently on her only for her to grab it and she took it beneath her head. I wish this night never gets over was in my mind.

The alarm rang at 8:00 and we got up and got ready for the final day. It was the most silent day of our entire training period as we never wanted to get things over. But as they say all good things come to an end so did this. We had our train at 8:00 and we went to the station and went to sleep at once as everyone was tired and had not slept last night. We did not get anytime to discuss anything, neither did anyone bothered.

Everyone has got something on this tour, Avinash and me got our friendship new dimension. Aarushi has got some moments she can cherish all her life. I almost have fallen for Aarushi but the star mark on our relationship was not acceptable to me. I did not reply to her proposal, but I was dying to say yes.

"Let me see what I can do for it, I said to myself as the train reached the New Delhi railway station.

We took our cabs to our home without saying anything to anyone.

Chapter 7

Confirmation

*"When we first kissed, that's when I
realized from then on that,
I did not want anybody else's lips on mine
But your's."*

One week passed after we returned from the training and we only contacted with each other through a common wtsapp group MUMBAI-unforgetable. We have completed our one year in the oragnisation and it was time for us to get our confirmation letters, Avinash got it a little earlier than us as his manager was more active when it comes to paperwork. However a week later we had our sales closing meeting and there for the first time I and Aarushi met after returning from Mumbai. Contrary to the previous experience of our teammates when we never used to talk each other we sat together in the meeting and gossiped before our manager announced,

"Let us all congratulate Aarushi and Jay for completion of the successful training period and now they are the confirmed employees of the organization".

Our national manager presented us with the confirmation letter and gave a nice speech appreciating me and Aarushi for doing an exceptional work without experience. This was the first company for me and Aarushi and that is why he used the phrase without experience. We were more than happy as everyone clapped for and it was a proud moment for both of us. Aarushi took no time to update about it on our wtsapp group. We three already had decided that we will celebrate only after all of us had our letters with us. So Avinash asked to come to Rajouri Garden after the meeting to celebrate it. The meeting got over at around 7 but I and Aarushi decided not to go together as it will give the office people a new matter to gossip. So I left for Rajouri with my bike and Aarushi took a cab to it. We reached the one-x mall and after 1 week we were again together, we hugged each other and ordered a cake. We cut it together and it was time for some dinner.

"What will you have" I asked, pointing to Aarushi and expecting an answer for Avinash.

"Chicken aur kya!" bingo Avinash replied and we all busted out in laughter and ordered chicken. Time and tide wait for none, is what I realized that because we were so busy talking to each other that the clock has moved four complete circles in between and what could have happened, yes Aarushi's phone rang as per schedule but contrary she did not pick it up.

"We should leave now" I said and paid the bill as quickly as possible.

"Madam ko pahucha dena hostle" (drop madam to hostle) Avinash said to me.

"Yes, I will and we booked a cab to the south –X New Delhi leaving my bike in the parking.

"My warden won't allow me to enter now it is too late", Aarushi said.

"So what next", I asked.

She paused for a few seconds and said,

"Can we stay in a hotel if you are ok with it".

"Are you sure?".

"Me and you one room".

"Yeah in Mumbai also we were together only so what's the problem.", she said.

Her phone started to ring again, "Mummy" what should I say?"

Just relax Aarushi say that you are on your way that's all and she did the same. Again, it rang,

"Abhishek", I was more than happy to see that Babu has been replaced by Abhishek in her contact list. With an overwhelmed smile, I said

"Tell him not to worry and you will reach in half an hour".

"He will kill me, you don't know him I cannot get pass his queries and in case I don't pick he will call the hostel warden".

I picked the phone and kept on her ear.

"I will be late in the office so talk to you tomorrow" Abhishek said and I could hear the voice outside the phone.

"Ok", she replied.

"Cheer up man now relax".

We started with our search of hotel only to get after answering around 200 questions as to what my and her relation was. It's been a pathetic experience and I was remembering the same people of Mumbai in other teams who questioned us. Anyhow, I got passed their questions and explained everything and they allowed us. We went to the room. She called her mother and I lite my cigarette just to observe her. After about half an hour she was done with her calls and came to lie down on one side of the bed and on the other side was me. We gazed at each other without a blink and all of a sudden moved at once just to kiss each other, we kissed again. Our lips holded us in the position. Her lips had a very unique fragrance of the gel she used. I kept kissing her hoding her from her waist before I regained my senses and gently pushed her.

"No Aarushi this is not right" I said, and moved back.

There was a moment of silence for a few minutes and then Aarushi busted out in a laugh.

"Look at your face you are so frightened Iay!"

I did not reply to her and went on to the chair and lighted my cigarette.

"This looks funny to you, I have never felt this before. It might not be a new thing for you since you are in a relationship since your childhood, but not me." I said blowing the puff in the air.

"I might be in a relationship, but I have not slept with him did you get that. You don't know why I did what I did, so don't assume. I love you and want to be with you that's all. I can't marry you because of some reason, but just because I can't marry does not mean I don't love you", she said all in one note and on a high pitch with added scream.

Then she did something which I have never have seen doing before, took a cigarette and light it up and started to smoke. Only after the first puff she started to cough like hell, easy, easy I rubbed her back as fast as possible.

"Please give me my bag", she said, pointing towards the table.

I gave her and she took out some pumping device and blew it in her mouth and regained her breath.

"What the hell is that?"

I am asthmatic so I use this pump.

"My god you never said anything about it".

"That's fine, no need to worry, I won't die, she said, and lyed in the bed. If possible don't light more cigarette she said as I took the stuff in my hand. I kept it aside and went on the bed just to rub her back as she was breathing at a higher than normal pace. She held my hand and placed her head in my lap.

"I love you", she said.

I was speechless for any answer as I was not clear as what should I do for this, so I shrugged all the thoughts running through me and switched off the light and went to sleep.

———— ◆ ————

Chapter 8

The Journey

"Time flies when you are there where you are Meant to be."

After that night, I decided that I won't bother her asking about marriage now onwards. And I decided to propose her. I called her one morning on a Sunday and we decided to meet at Connaught place at 12:00. I reached there and finished my smoking work quickly because I was frightened that if this creature will join me in this, then it will spoil my entire planning. I was not a dude kind of guy so there was nothing very innovative I could think of. I just mugged few lines to propose her which was used by one of friends in our school. I was waiting at the restaurant in the metro station and there she comes wearing a beautiful brown suit with laces on the front side. It was very prompt as I thought it will easy to open her laces, this is cheap and vulgar you are not that kind, I said to myself and threw away all the thoughts aside.

"Hi, how are you? Looking good" she said.

"I look good on Sundays because I take bath on Sunday for sure", I said in reply and we smiled together.

"So what will you have I asked as courteously as I hardly cared about the answer because of the butterflies in my stomach.

"Cool Blue", she replied.

"What's that I asked". It is a drink, let me bring it for both of us.

There it is she comes back with two glasses of some blue water kind of thing. I always had this perception that these brands just sell water by adding different colors in it and some added flavours, which any one make at home also. Anyhow, what I have to do with it, let me do my work I said to myself and started.

"Aarushi I have to propose you", I said.

And she laughed and continued for a few minutes. I was not sure as to what made her laugh, but I waited for her to get normal.

"Do it, I am listening", she said.

I went blank as to what to say, this has happened to me all my life whenever I have mugged up anything during my exams I had also never delivered them, but any how you cannot take chit paper in your examination hall, but here I was allowed to do so and I took out the piece of paper on which I have written my lines.

"Read it, I sat and passed the paper to her.

She read it, this is not the way to propose, you need to do the drill. What's the meaning of drill, I asked.

"Don't you watch movies, you need bend down on your knees and recite these lines."

I looked around the restaurant looked very crowded. I can't do that you have read the lines and I think that is what proposal is all about, to say your feelings to the concerned person.

"Ok then", she said and started to drink the blue water that was kept on the table.why these people only observe only idiotic things in movies. I could not figure out what to say, so I just held her hand, looked into her eyes and said:

I was waiting for you,
I was dying for you,
At last I found you,
I LOVE YOU.

"Repeat it once again, I was waiting for you I was dying for you at last I found you, I love you too" she said before I could complete.

"Yes!", I shouted just to get everyone's attention. I have got this habit of getting attention from strangers everytime I am in a crowded place.

"Sry, sry guys" I said just to get away from the stare from everyone and sit back. We smiled, looking at each other and next few hours passed talking useless stuffs but was more of which an effort from both of us to spend more time together.

The clock ticked 6 and it was time I should drop her back to her hostel, so we took the metro and reached the INA metro station just to realize at the exit, that it is more than 7 hours we have spent inside the metro without exit which is an offence. The police over there took us to the metro officials and they did their inquiry for more than 2 hours before they came to the conclusion that we do not belong to any terrorist group. We both got to sign a written apology for them as a promise not to repeat the same offense again in the future and we paid the penalty as well. However, we reached the hostel and against our will we both needed to get separated for next few hours.

"Time flies when you are alive"

The next few months flew like anything, we used to talk whole night and only did we kept our phone down was when I reached her hostel. There was nothing much to talk between us still the silence on the phone was more to say than the words from the mouth. This went around for 8 months and in the process our performance in the organization went down drastically, which the organization cannot afford. We both got a number of reminders to improve our performance, but we were so deeply into each other than we did not take a heed of it. And finally we got a termination letter as an offer on the new years eve.

It was not a shock to either of us, but anyhow we decide that we did not need to worry and we will find some other job. We both gave interview in different companies and regained our places with a better package much to the relief of Aarushi because I hardly cared about the package but about the different companies that we have got selected. We started to work in our respective organization and decided that we will focus more on work and will only talk to each other in the evening after our work. The bondage was getting stronger day by day and none of us could ever imagine that both of us were strangers few months back. Not even in the wildest of my dreams ever a thought crossed my mind that this may ever end. But the destiny has other plans.

Chapter 9

Journey Meets Destination

"And suddenly,
We were strangers again!"

Cardiovascular disease has become a very prevailing event in Indian society these days, and more common to the fathers of the pretty girls of the society. I think someone needs to work out on the fact, and I am very sure it is a fact, to find out that which gods in the ancient civilization have cursed the fathers of pretty girls to suffer from heart disease. And even a minor problem of high BP which can be because of eating unhealthy food items will result in heart attack is what every girl believes. So nothing new to my experience as I got a call one afternoon, one day when I was in the office that Aarushi's dad has got a heart attack and she needs to go urgently to Lucknow. I did not know what to say, but still uttered what ritual says,

"Everything will be fine, Aarushi, don't worry".

"I have booked my tickets to Lucknow, the flight is scheduled at 6 in the evening."

"I will reach there don't worry", I replied, dropping the phone.

I completed my work and went to the airport just to see her off. She looked highly terrified and I just consoled her before she went to board the plane.

As soon I reached my home, I got a call from her I have reached and will get in touch with you as soon as I get free. I said ok as I was very confident that this is a very common phenomenon and her father hardly will take a day or 2 to get well.

2 days went back and I did not hear anything from her, I was busy but very nervous at times. I hope everything is well is what I was telling to myself. I was not able to sleep and was roaming inside my room just to figure out as to what must have happened and why the hell she is not calling me. I was checking my phone as many times as possible, wtsapp says last seen 2 days back status. I was really worried, but anyhow I tried to get myself under control took some sleeping pills and went on to sleep. I got up the next morning and the first thing I did was check my phone for any calls or message. Aarushi tagged you in a photo was a message from Facebook, I thanked Mark Zuckerberg for the wonderful platform he has created for getting in touch with each other. I opened the app and saw her picture with Abhishek holding each other hands, and the status says "Journey Meets Destination", it was an engagement picture. I was shocked did not know how to react and all I could do was went out of my bed and threw my phone to a distant wall with full force, went down on my knees and then on the ground and busted out with tears. I cried out loud hitting the surface as it was the culprit of all the events. I just could not control off, hitting everything in

the ground, the bed the walls, the door only to realize that I have broken my toe in all this process. It was hurting like anything but more painful was the status, journey meets destination. Things started to disappear and I was completely blank, I could not understand as what I should do in this situation as now I do not have the phone so that I can call anyone, I have a broken finger so I could not walk and I have lost my love Aarushi. Life has come to a stand still for me and I was just crying, sitting at one place in the corner of my room. All the moments that we have spent together were passing through my head and made my condition worse, and the immense pain of the broken toe took me to an unconscious state.

———◆———

Chapter 10

The Saviour

"The greatest gift my parents gave me, my BROTHER He sees my best, he sees my worst He sees my lows, he sees my highs But through all these days, he always stand's by."

Like everyone I also have that one person who is always present beside me like an angel every time I am in some trouble. My younger brother Vicky. He is a final year student in one the engineering colleges situated in Noida. He stays there in the college hostel and visited me every weekend just to meet me, so that we can spend some time together. But his visit today was not as usual as when I regained my consciousness, I just saw him sitting with tears in his eyes and rubbing his hands on my head.

"What has happened to you", he asked me showing the broken phone and looking at me.

"Nothing, just that I was playing football I collided with the wall and I have broken my finger, pointing to the finger of my leg" I said.

"What, have you gone mad or what?", he shouted before he went and bought an auto and took me to the hospital.

The next few minutes were very painful before I finally had some pain killer injection and bandage around my broken finger. We came back home and had some food which he ordered online. I ate a little bit of it and left everything on the plate. I took a cigarette and light it up and went to sleep in a very short period of time as the sedatives started to do its work.

I woke up the next morning just to see Aarushi and Vicky sitting together and talking. She directly came from the airport to this place as everything must have been informed by my brother to her. I did not utter a single word or asked any question and just started to cry watching her hands which was decorated by Mehndi. They both ran together to hug me and we cried all at once not knowing who is crying for what. But I was sure for myself that I cried because I lost my love Aarushi.

"Why have you come here, please leave", I said regaining my breaths.

"I will explain you everything don't get me wrong, let me speak, Aarushi replied.

"I don't need any explanation, please leave now. Just go away from here and never ever show me your face, you are a liar and a cheater. You betrayed me, my love and everything. She left with tears.

"She is a cheater Vicky, don't talk to her ever in life, she lied to me", I said all at once just hugging my brother.

I mailed to my manager regarding the broken finger with a leave application only to get a reply that I was not a confirm employee till now and he cannot give me leave and in the process I was terminated from my post. The pain of loosing my love was so big that all these things hardly mattered to me at that moment.

I informed Vicky everything because I knew he is the one who can take me out of these things. Everything has come to an end for me all at once, I was not sure as what to do now. I was missing Aarushi like anything so was she. She kept calling my brother as many times possible just to get my information. She tried to talk to me also but I refused.

There has been events in the past with my friends who have lost their love and I have dealt with them, consoled them and made them realize that this life is much more than that one person but not today. I was at the receiving end and then only I realized that it sucks,it is sad. It is lonely, it is heart breaking, it is life changing. It is tragic, it is pathetic, it is devastating, it is depressing… She has left a void that can never be filled because there is no body else I could ever love. I missed her probably more than anyone in this entire world.

Two months passed by I kept deteriorating my mental status. I have become so used to and obsessed with her that days went like decades to me and even after putting a lot of effort I was not able to come out of her. I have never been in this status before and so my brother started to panic and decided to inform my parents.

"I am going to call mummy here, she can take better care of you", Vicky said.

"Not at all, she will panic more and, will make the condition worse, I will get well don't worry", I said and begged at the same time not to inform.

You need to put an effort to get well and start to focus on your career."

I will do that, I replied with a full energetic gesture. I will go and meet some of my friends and find some reference to get a job, I said to my brother hugging.

All these efforts I have put just to show that I am getting well and ready to face the challenges as I thought my brother has started to get frustrated watching me all day in the bed and crying. There are times in your life when the strongest pillar finds it difficult to support you, and prays for you to get well. That was what my brother was doing for me.

I took my bike and went to a near by Gururdwara, as I thought that my religion gods have stopped listening to me and I should try other places and religion to get Aarushi. There was nothing in my mind except Aarushi and all I wanted was her. This routine continued with me for the next few days, I got up to get ready and went to the same Gurudwara and spent the entire day praying and doing all the stuffs that people visiting over there did. Against my hardcore belief, nothing changed, I was still in a depressed stage just wandering here and there, but from deep inside I was looking for Aarushi.

It cannot go the same way, I was man of value and that the greatest and most idiotic value that I carried was not to ask for money from my dad. I decided to apply for the job as the savings I was drying up and in that case I will need to ask for money from dad, which may result him knowing everything, and that will be more painful than my current situation as my dad was strict when it comes to career. Contrary to the popular belief, Finding jobs is comparatively an easier task when it comes to sales, because of new ventures and startup companies growing at a faster rate in India. So I uploaded my resume on different websites and got an offer as a marketing manager in a nearby hospital. I informed about this to my brother and we celebrated as I have become the CEO of Apple.

Chapter 11

Compulsive Obsessive Disorder

"There is someone for every person and
The person for you is a psychiatrist."

I joined the hospital and after completing my one week training I started my field work. I have never got an opportunity to work in an office all my life till now, but to be very frank I never wanted it though. Office work is highly overrated as I thought that field work always gives you the opportunity to meet new people and explore different things. In the office, all you get is to sit at one place and see the same faces and same routine, but people can argue about this and but currently I am not in a mental status to discuss all this, I said to one of my colleague. I completed my one month over there and got my salary credited on the first of the next month. Much to my relief as I did not need to borrow any money what so ever to pay the rent and all the stuffs from my dad. I decided to purchase a new phone with it as I was fed up of using the smaller version. I will have an i-Phone I said to myself and went on to purchase it. Thanks to Steve Jobs for blessing us with such a gadget and to the banks for the credit they provide because it was not possible to purchase a costly gadget as i-Phone at one go with the amount that is credited in our account in the form of salary. So I had this new I phone with me and it gave me my little swag which I had before as I thought it is the best phone anyone can have on planet earth right now and I am one of the luckiest person. So I put my sim in the new phone and downloaded the apps as per my requirement. The companies these days want their employees to have wtsapp installed on their phone at any cost so that they can pass all the useless and sometimes useful information through it. I downloaded the app and did all the formalities only to see that I have 23400 wtsapp messages on to it, 21368 of them from one single person, Aarushi. I love you was the only message she typed, 21368 times. Has she gone mad or what I thought to myself, but still decided to reply. You are a liar and a cheater.

"You have betrayed me and you will be never be happy all your life I curse you", I wrote and sent and then blocked her like a teenager. I was angry as hell but still controlled my urge to throw the phone as it was a costly gadget and I have still not paid for it. I had my dinner and completed all the office work and decide to sleep. I have been taking these sleeping pills for quite some time now, so I took them and went in my bed. Although I tried to control but still could not and opened my Facebook account just to see Aarushi profile. Aarushi Abhishek Singh, her name was updated. As I scrolled down Aarushi has uploaded 123 pictures of the wedding with the status "TOGETHER FOREVER" and

I did not stop there scrolled down, Aarushi Abhishek Singh checked in with Abhishek Singh in honeymoon resort, Goa. Tears started to roll down my eyes as I gently kept the phone aside and hid myself inside the sheet and cried and end up sleeping in no time as I had taken the pills before.

Morning, I got up with a heavy head and without any enthusiasm for the work, but still pushed myself and went. Through the entire day the only thought I had in my mind what Aarushi would have been doing now. This very thought pushed me again and again to visit her profile on Facebook.

Everytime I visited her profile she shared something or the other as she wanted me to know everything she did. But none of them were to my likings as all the pictures featured Abhishek and Aarushi holding each other. I started to get depressed again and was not sure as to what should I do to cope with it. My new job has given a lot of responsibility to me and I cannot quit that also. I was not sure as to what life wanted from me or I may say what Aarushi wanted. I was not sure as to whom should I discuss all this because I have to get out of it at any cost. This very thought of Aarushi started to take my all attention and I was not able to figure out to what I should do until one day I was roaming in the hospital in the afternoon and I saw one board, Department of Mental Health Sciences and a lot of people waiting outside the doctors chambers. Are these many people in the process of becoming mad was the first thought that passed my mind. So I waited there as to see what is going to happen when the doctors arrived. There were lots of junior doctors who were talking to the people one at a time and asking about the problems they are facing. I was very surprised to see that most of them were ladies who had some problem or the other in their household. There were small kids also, I could not figure out as to what must have happened to them as they were too young for any problem of mental health, but still the doctors treated with the utmost care and all their forms were filled after asking certain questions. The doctor arrived after a few minutes and people were called in one by one in the chamber and contrary to my experience here the doctor took a lot of time with each patient. I guess he must have been listening to each one of them and their stories before coming to any conclusion. I sat there for 5 hours just watching all the process as I thought that as I will reach home, I will start browsing social network and something will definitely add to my depression. All the patients were done and the doctor left, leaving behind a lot of paper work for the junior doctors.

Suddenly I heard a voice from behind "Excuse me!", and I turned to see a pretty lady with a smile. "Yes please" I replied. "You are sitting here for quite some time, are you ok", she asked. I did not know that somebody was observing me, but still I replied,

"Yeah, I am waiting for Dr Batra, I had to discuss something, I work over here as a marketing manager" pointing to the ID I said just to make sure that she don't conclude me ISI agent.

"Dr Batra came and left you did not notice", she said with a smile.

"You were busy watching our procedures I guess".

Yeah, all these people are suffering from mental disorders I asked just to shift the topic.

She smiled and said "No, no they are not suffering from mental disorders but they have some initial symptoms like sadness, confused thinking etc." Most of them come just to take advice on their current status, she said completing her sentence. Listening to the symptoms as shared by this pretty lady added to my curiosity as I thought that these symptoms resembles that of mine. However, I could not grasp enough courage to share this because it may just be my assumptions and nothing else. She went back to join the other doctors and I carried on my way back to home as it was already too late in the evening.

The next few days the only thought that kept my mind occupied that "Am I suffering from mental disorder?" because the symptoms the doctor shared with me were matching that of mine. I was restless, for sleep I needed pills and thought of what Aarushi must be doing kept haunting me. I have began to cry a lot and retreat into myself rather being social and open. I was lonely and miserable and how hard I may try but could not regain the feeling of life being beautifull. I felt like something has crawled in my mind an flipped off all the positive switches and switched on all the negative ones. I felt hopeless and it was more of disease than feeling. However, I was not sure as whether I should consult the doctor or not. I had a feeling that it will give me a lable of being mad, which I never wanted to be. Half knowledge is always a dangerous act as I believed that going to psychologist means I have become mad and I will be admitted in the mental asylum. This thought prevented me from taking any action and stopped even to consult a doctor. However the days passed by and my mental condition was getting horrible and I was not able to concentrate on my work and I started to fight with the pears around me and the family members for unknown reasons. My performance was degrading day by day and I was only worried about, what Aarushi must be doing now. We didn't talk last six months and it has really started to haunt me.

I was called by the manager for evaluating my performance and he literally thrashed me with his words and gave a final warning to improve my performance otherwise I will be terminated. I came out of the meeting hall depressed and light my energy booster. The first thought that came to my mind was to get out of depression, because this way I can't be all my life. I cant allow one single person or event to decide the fate of my life and I decided to meet the psychologist. Next day, my only objective was to meet the doctor and I booked my appointment. I was there in the hospital when I saw the pretty doctor whom I have talked earlier.

I went to her and said, "Can you do me a favour?".

"What you want me to do?" she asked.

"I have booked an appointment with the doctor today, but I don't want to discuss with him as he is too senior and he will get the wrong idea about me.

She smiled and said, "Is she married or ditched you?" I was astonished to hear the question as to what should I answer because she was married and she ditched me to marry, so both the condition applied but still replied "Both". I was figuring it out in my mind as to how she knew about all this, but before I could conclude anything she asked

"Ok, now what favour you want from me?".

"I want to consult you about my problem, because I think you are around my age and better equipped to understand me, look how spontaneously you judged me", I said just trying to praise her and convince her to look into my case.

"Ok then you need to meet me after 7, because I can't give you consultation till the doctor leaves. I was fine with it and said yes. I went with my work just trying to engage and pass the time till the clock hits 7. At around 7, I went to the department just to see the doctor was getting ready to leave and I waited for him to leave as I did not want to face him at any cost.

"Dr Aditi is calling you in her chamber", an old nurse said to me. That was the first time I got to know that the doctor name was Aditi. I went to her chamber and she just made me sit on a relaxing chair and added some equipments on different areas of my body. I was terrified as to what she is going to do with me, but still kept silence and waited for her to finish. The doctors have been blessed with the intuition to know exactly what the patient is thinking, "You don't need to worry, this is just to check your pulse rate and emotional status while you talk with me", she said looking at me.

"Ok, that's fine" I replied.

We began the session and I narrated the entire story to her in one go, without her asking anything.

Tears kept rolling down my eyes and I kept on narrating the entire story to her and she did not stop neither I nor she tried to wipe my tears off. I completed my story and without hearing anything from her took all the stuffs out of my body and went out of the room. I was shivering and crying and straight on went to the cigarette shop to take a smoke.Before I could finish my stuff a car stopped in front of me and Dr. Aditi came out of it.

"Call me once you feel like talking", she said, handing over her business card. I did not reply to her and she left.

The next few days went by and I did not meet the doctor and neither did I call her I was feeling embarrassed as I thought a man should never cry, it is a sign of weakness and that also in front of a lady is horrible. However, one day in the afternoon I received a call from her

"Hey, Jay how are you I am Dr Aditi got your number from the marketing department", she said.

"I am fine" I said in reply.

"You will have to come and meet me in the evening", "ok", I replied as I did not have anything else to say at that point to me. I went to meet her and she explained about the analysis and interpretation she has gained by listening to my story. You know it is a very common mental disorder these days and I will help you come out of it.

What disorder I said, jumping out of my chair, "Have I gone mad?" I said.

"No, all mental disorders did not end up in madness, did you get that she said with a loud voice. Just sit and listen to me first. I was bit terrified hearing that voice.

"So what is it?" I asked her.

"You know everything that you do revolve around one thing",

"What?" I asked her.

"Aarushi!" She replied and stood up.

"In medical terms, this is termed as OCD".

"OCD? What's that?" I asked her.

"Obsessive Compulsive Disorder", she said, and sat on the chair beside me.

"It is a very common disorder and you will get out of it, I will help you in this" she said and continued

"More often than not, we misinterpret the empty feeling we feel inside. Sometimes when the humans feel sad they blame the external factors before they realize that actually they the ones who created the sadness itself. Then you say that you miss the person so much and will do any thing to get them back but from you just know it is not possible".

"Will I be normal or not?", I asked her as I did not had any answer to that intellect.

"You are perfectly normal, just that your mind is over occupied with Aarushi which is reducing your productivity in everything you do", she said calming me down.

"All you need to do is to meet me everyday or talk on the phone at whatever time you are comfortable", she said consoling the terrified mind.

"I want to be normal, Aditi please help me in this" I begged her as done by any kid.

"You will be fine", she replied.

———————◆———————

Chapter 12

Recuperate

"To heal a wound, you should stop touching it."

I thank god for blessing me with such a great luck that every time I am in some pain he sends someone or the other to take me out of that trouble, I said to Aditi as the session for the day completed. It has been 15 days since I am visiting you for my illness and now I am in a much better shape when it comes to mental status. You need to follow the instructions and visit the same way as you did for last 15 days, Aditi said handing me a written instruction. But how much more time will it take, as I am feeling quite well as of now.

"It will take at least 3 more months for you to be completely normal, if you do as I say or you will get mad", she said with a smile.

"I am not charging you anything but you never bothered to ask me for a coffee, you are so mean and miser" she said just locking the door of her chamber.

"I thought, many a times, but did not because I thought you may take it otherwise". I said to her.

"No, I won't take otherwise, let's go" she said and we both started to move into a luxurious coffee shop in the hospital. Corporate hospitals in today's era are just like shopping malls they have all the stuffs right from coffee shops to bookstores and garments and everything. It hardly gives you a feeling of a hospital where sick people are. Contrary to our B town hospitals where the majority of people is seen crying and yelling and a lot of unnecessary crowd. Here there are a limited number of people allowed as visitor with each patient and proper hygiene is maintained. However, I was not in a condition to worry about country problems right now as I myself was ill and needed to sort that out first. I took a seat in front of the lady doctor with a gentle smile.

"What will you have?" I asked.

"Nutty fudge brownie, Gourmet hot chocolate",

"What what?" I asked as I have never heard the name before.

These all the things are also served here, I did not know. I only knew cappuccino. And she busted out in laughter. I have met her from quite some time now, but I have never seen that laughter on her face, all she had was a habit of smiling and nothing else. However, I was glad to see my ignorance bought a laughter to her face. I went to order with the menu and pointed out the things she asked for as I thought I will not be able to pronounce them correctly. You almost know everything about me, but I don't know whatsoever anything about you except that you are a doctor, I said as I took a sip of the hot stuff from the cup.

"What you want to know about me, you can ask anything", she said in between her drinks. I was surprised to hear the answer and started to wonder as to what should I ask, as I was not sure whether we are sitting here professionally or I can go with the some personal conversation.

"Anything means anything", she said as she analysed the dilemma I was going through.

"How many brothers and sisters do you have?", I asked just to make her laugh once again and she could not control it for a minute or two.

"This is what you wanted to know about me", she said trying to hold her laughter. "I am not able to figure as to what I should ask, so…" I replied feeling very stupid in front of her.

I am the only daughter to my parents, my father is a businessman and mother is a lawyer AND I DON'T HAVE A BOYFRIEND. She said in one go controlling the laugh and started to drink her stuff. That's cool Aditi, quite a rich and highly educated family.

"Yes, you can say but because of all these stuffs everyone is mostly busy in their work and we are hardly getting family time. Dad is out most of the time on his business trips and mom busy with her clients and I stay most of the time in the hospital because I don't want to be alone."

I don't have much of friends also with whom I can gossip and share my things, so I have decided to dedicate time mostly in studies. You know I have 2500 books in my library and I have read most of them. All these seem like a fantasy to me as I have been born and brought up in a middle class family and a library with 2500 books is unimaginable to me. I was not sure as these many books do really exist also. And how can anybody read these many books. We hardly could read the subject books and books other than subjects did not have any relevance to me. All these seemed to me a fairy tale and I began to imagine the place where all have been kept together. However, I did not want to look stupid again so I just praised for the collection that she had and casually asked if I could see her library once.

"Come with me today only I will show you my library", she said finishing her coffee.

"No, not today as it is too late and you must also be tired", I said just to get away with the situation as I was not sure to visit her place and thinking of what people will make out of it.

"Ok, then Sunday you are invited for lunch at my home", she said, grasping her keys and leather purse lying on the table.

"Are you sure?", I just asked as I was not sure about it.

"I am pretty sure and you are coming no excuses", she said as we reached the parking area.

"Ok", I replied as did not have anything else to say.

"Bye then meets you tomorrow she said as she started her car engine and flew. I started my bike and went to the near by shop for a smoke, a thought struck me, "I don't have a boyfriend", Aditi said to me but why? Girls, I believe always gives something or the other to guess about them, but anyhow, I don't need to think all this I said to myself and stopped all the thoughts before they could take control over my mind and lighted my cigarette.

I went back home and completed all my office work. I received a message from my immediate manager, congratulation you have achieved your target for the month, well done. I was very happy to read the message as after a long time I have applauded for my work.

I replied "thank you", to my boss not much to my liking, but just an obedient gesture. I must thank Aditi as because of her I am now able to perform well. I forwarded the message from the boss with a caption

"This is all because of you, thank you".

"Congratulations, and party tomorrow from your end", she replied.

"Done" I replied back and I switched off my phone as instructed by my doctor. No phone at night and no social network "To heal the wound you should stop touching the wound", was the first instruction she gave me when she started my treatment. Now I did not need sleeping pills and also have developed a strong will power to throw away all the thoughts of Aarushi as soon as they come in my mind.

Chapter 13

A New Beginning

"Take a leap of faith and dive into the ocean for who has made us, has made the ocean. If he has guided us to the ocean, he must have planned our survival. New beginning always starts with closed doors, What may look an end to us is actually a new beginning."

Time changes everything, it changes you, your wounds are healed, your attitude, so it changes the people around you. Three months have passed since I began my treatment and it is about to finish tomorrow. I have developed an attitude of confidence, started to perform in the organization and moreover, I have started to love myself. My behavior towards friends and family has been reestablished and everyone seems to be happy seeing me as I used to be. I am thankful to you Aditi for doing all this, you really have saved me. I was almost out of control of my mind and heart and my life, you took the pain out of all busy schedules to take care of me, thank you for everything. I said as we finished the final session for the treatment of my illness. So now you are free and completely fine. I smiled and thanked her again.

"But now for all the services that I have rendered you I will charge you".

I was surprised to hear this and my account balance started to roll back in my head. I stopped my thought process just to grasp her attention and showing I am not worried at all hearing about the fees.

"Yeah, tell me what I need to do."

"What can you do for me?

"I don't know you only have to tell me.

"Ok, lets go to the coffee shop and I will tell you what I want.

We moved to the coffee shop with a puzzled mind as I was not able to figure it out, as to what she may ask. Anyhow, I collected all the procastration and ordered the drinks as per likings and said

"Yes, please tell me what should I do?"

You know Jay, it may sound very unusual to you, but I have started to develop a feeling for you, I don't know why, but you have started to occupy my mind more than anything else. Are you getting what I want to say?

"Have your cup of coffee, I said, pouring the sugar in her cup and stirring the spoon.

I started before she could utter anything else, Aditi look just today I have recovered from illness of OCD in your language. I was over occupied with one thought, now you are trying to go into that stage. With due respect to all the feelings of yours and extra mile you have travelled to make me come out of my illness, I request you to please put aside any thoughts whatsoever about this. You know, let's not complicate our chemistry, we are very good friends and lets be like that as of now. I may have got over all my thoughts about Aarushi but still, my heart beats for her only and I don't think I will be able to do any justice to any other relation.

"But she left you and married someone else and still you are talking about her".

That has nothing to do with my love for her, she was free to choose, to love whoever she wanted and I am free to love whoever I want and I choose her. You are one of the best persons I have ever met with a kind heart and great soul. Relation can complicate our lives, so let's choose to be great friends, please I don't have any intention to lose a person as well as you. I said completing my sentence.

We both moved into silence mode for the next couple of minutes before Aditi started to speak breaking the monotony.

"Will you come to meet me everyday?" She asked with a gentle smile.

"If you want I can stay at your place", I replied and we both laughed, which somewhat reduced the tension in the air surrounding us.

"So now my fees".

"Yes, what I have to do", I asked.

"All you need is to meet me in the morning, have lunch with me and meet me before you leave the hospital."

I smiled at her and said ok, as you say.

Since I had been following the guidelines of Aditi from the past three months, so I decided to continue the same process. I started my day by meeting her at the hospital and after that work and everything else as instructed by her. She used to bring delicious lunch for both of us everyday and I used to join their bunch of doctors of department of mental health sciences. We started to get into a different bondage with time. We started to spend more and more time together and getting to know each other. Time seemed to flourish and flow like the blink of an eye and one year passed. You never get to know how really time works, when things are good and in your favour it flows at such a pace. But you realize it once it is time for departure. With the splendid performance I had in my organization over a year I was promoted as manager and transferred to Banglore. This news came to me as a shock rather than a surprise because after hearing this the first thought that crossed my mind as to how Aditi is going to react. Promotion, salary hike everything else took a back seat. I was not sure as to what should I say to her about this. A gentle fear of losing her started to grasp my attention as I was frightened to imagine a day without her. There was no feeling of love, but fear of losing a great friend.

Anyhow, you need to be strong to face all the challenges, you need to feed the beast Jay I said to myself and decided to tell her the next day. The next morning I called her to meet early at the coffee shop at sharp 8, two hours before her daily OPD timings started. I thought this much time would be enough to make her understand everything. By the time I reached, Aditi was already there. The coffee shop by then have understood what our likings were and bought the hot stuffs before even I was settled in the chair. I have to tell you something, I have been promoted as a manager in my organization. She just stood up from her chair and hugged me,

"Congratulations!". I always knew something very good is coming your way.

But the sad part is that,

"What is the sadd part she completed before I could speak. Tell me what the hell is the sad part".she asked with a louder voice.

"I have been transferred to Banglore", I said.

Pin drop silence from her side no expressions, she just left the cup on the table and went out without saying anything. I did not get the courage to follow her. I always knew that she won't appreciate this, but the way she reacted was also not known to me. I had planned to make her understand that although I may be leaving the city, but we will keep in touch as we are now but I did not get an opportunity about all this. Just that I was trying to figure out as to how I should approach her and make her understand all this I received a call from my manager. He asked me to come to the office and complete all the formalities before leaving. Without giving any second thought, I went to the office where all the seniors have gathered together to applaud and congratulate me. I was given my official promotion and transfer letter before I was told that I need to join the new place in three days time. I did not have much to say to any of them as I hardly cared. The appreciation session completed in the evening and I went back home as fast as possible. I was in a hurry to call and talk to Aditi and make her understand all this.

"The mobile you are trying to call has been switched off was the reply from the generous computer lady after 2 hours and 30 calls on a repeated note.

I was not able to figure it out as to what should I do now, as I was getting desperate to talk to Aditi. The clock hit 12 and now I felt that I have only 1 day to make her understand, earlier, which looked to me a 2 hour job now one day was not looking good enough for the same activity. I will meet her tomorrow in the hospital and make her understand everything, I decided before going to sleep. I was desperate for the night to get over, but they all had planned to stay longer today. Thoughts were rolling one after the other finding out a solution or an idea which will help me to come out of the situation and in the process when did I surrender myself to sleep was not known.

Next morning, I got up and rushed to the hospital to meet Aditi but in vain.

"She is on a leave for a week, said one of the staff members outside her chamber.

I tried her phone just to hear the same repeated voice of the lady. Now the things started to darken in front of me because all the resources to meet and talk to her have put a sign of OUT OF ORDER right now. I could not do anything else and decided to wait till I got a call from her. Next morning, I had the flight to Banglore, so I packed all the stuffs and got ready for the new destination. All the excitement of promotion and new profile has just vanished from my mind and with a heavy heart and puzzled mind, I closed my eyes before the flight took the pace on the runway and left the surface.

Chapter 14

Missing

"I Know miles and distance are the units of measurement, but   the units don't have the capacity to measure the distance I am feeling with you at this place. But who is going to explain it you, I don't know, all I know is that I MISS YOU....."

The games of life are not won by weak players, you need to be stronger and passionate for your win. Weakness is a sign of losers and I never wanted to be one, but as I had started to get rewarded in the eyes of the society, parents and everyone there are many more things I was lost in the process not known to anyone. First Aarushi left without explaining anything and now Aditi. It was hard for me to figure it out as to whether I am a winner or a loser.

However, the city of Banglore welcomed me with shower. It is one of the finest cities in India. From amazing skyscrapers to greenery and from technies to friendly people. It has maintained its undamaged history and culture. Bangalore is also known as the garden city of India with clean and green atmosphere. The roads, parks, gardens are clean with almost no slums around. It is known as the IT capital of India, which is very much visible when you drive through the roads. I was surprised to know that more than 50k IT companies operate from here. The weather was also amazing, unlike Delhi, where it is too hot in summers and extremely cold during winters Banglore maintains a pretty similar climate throughout the year. Everything was amazing about the place and within a week I got totally acclimatize to the new change.

The team I received was also great and began to work more effectively getting to learn everyday as I was in a new role. Aditi kept on popping in my head every now and then, but she only had taught me how to control those thoughts during my illness which I was using against her. However, I kept on trying to contact her everyday, but without any clues.

I tried to be brave and throw away all the thoughts. We were friends and it is not only whole and sole responsibility of mine to reach her but same applies to her also. So why should I worry, when she had decided to escape from me, why should I chase her, were the things I repeated in my mind lying on the bed. After a very long time since the departure of Aarushi I was feeling lonely and alone. Right from the time I started my treatment I had always shared everything to Aditi. All those times I faced a lot of trouble, but was never worried because she used to take care of all the things and help me out of all problems. But now is the time when I am doing well and growing exponentially I am not able to share my feelings with the only person whom

I wanted to share Aditi. She must be in a lot of pain since my departure and I want to help her out was the second thought, that popped out of the innocent and confused mind.

"But how? I do not have any clue whatsoever of her and how can anyone help someone who is escaping."

The thoughts kept on coming one after the other like waves of water on the sea shore leaving their footprints and walk away. I started to get restless and heart started to beat at a faster rate. I cannot quit every time a thought came into my mind like a tsunami, I had quit on Aarushi, she came to me to explain why she did what she did, but I refused to hear her and now Aditi is doing the same thing she is refusing me. "NO, NO", I can't keep on loosing people because of my personal gains, "I have to find her at any cost", I said to myself and got out of the bed.

It was 2 o'clock at night, which was an appropriate time to write an application for a leave because no one going to read it right now and by the time they did, I will out of the town. All my life I have learned "suffering from fever" was the only reason I had given to take a leave, but not this time because "fever" won't allow and give me the luxury to leave the headquarter. So what else I can do to run away from the city. I will have to kill, yes, I will have to kill someone but whom? All the people are very dear to me. I will kill someone who is already dead, yeah, that will be fine. That will be a good idea because that won't hurt anyone and I will not have any guilt also. I wrote an application killing my grand mom who was already in the heavens and gave all the necessary reasons as to why it is urgent for me to go. I booked the earliest flight in the morning before my seniors can even get up from their bed and left the city.

———◆———

Chapter 15

The storyteller

"No matter how dark things may get into a story I feel it is the responsibility of the storyteller to leave the audience with a shred of hope. JOSH RADNOT"

"Please take care of your parents and yourself, we stand with you at this point of time and in case you need any help and support feel free to call", was the message I received from my boss as soon as the flight landed the Delhi airport.

"Thank you, sir, will come back as soon as possible", I texted him back.

I got out of the airport and booked the cab straight to the hospital and rushed to her chamber. There was some other doctor's name written on the door.

"Aditi madam kaun se chamber me hai" (Dr Aditi is available in which chamber) I asked one of the lady coordinators of the hospital.

"She has left the hospital", was her reply.

"What, where she works now", I asked her as I started to panic.

"I don't know, sir, you can get the details from the hospital management. I was in a rush as the adrenaline has started to secrete more in my body and heart has started to beat as I was participating in a 100m race.

"Excuse me, which hospital did Dr Aditi join after leaving from here", I asked the gentleman sitting in a closed glass chamber.

"Have a seat, sir, please fill this form as we do not give information to any unknown person", was his reply. I knew these idiots won't give the information without me filling up the form. These corporate hospitals don't give permission to meet our own family members without form fill up so it will be useless to fight for it. I did not waste any time and filled the form and handed over to him. He started to work on his computer as he was doing a research work in finding out the details. I kept my patience and waited for him to reply, although it was difficult.

"She had not left any information, I am sorry", was his reply after completing his NASA project to launch a satellite. The first thought that came to my mind was to punch him in his face for taking so much time with no information but I had a different goal so I said "Thank you", and left the chamber. A sudden fear and anxiety started to rush through my mind and thoughts of what all may go wrong started to occupy my mind. I don't need to panic and I will have to find her at any cost I said to myself blowing the hazardous smoke in the air. I will meet the most senior doctor of her department, which I was frightened till now. She must have told him and taken the advice before joining any new hospital. Yeah, he must be knowing about her. But what should I say if he asks me as to why I wanted to know about her, a thought rushed to my mind before I could feel better. All I will tell him is that I am his patient and needed to consult her. Yeah, that will be a good answer, ok let me wait for him and meet him in the evening.

"Smoking is injurious to health and when combined with tea it worsen the situation, people of your generation don't take care of your health" said one of the oldies sitting beside me at the tea stall just in front of the hospital.

"Yeah uncle, I know, but right now my mind has freaked out and I hardly care about my health." I replied.

"I know right now you are in a lot of pain and something has occupied your mind more than anything else." Said the old man.

"Yeah! But how do you know?", I asked anxiously.

"Because you are drinking tea from both the glasses one of which is mine", he said with a smile on his face.

I looked at both the sides and found them half empty.

"I am sorry uncle, I will pay for both of them and will buy one for you. I am very sorry", I said, feeling apologetic to him.

"It's ok beta, no problem", he said generously.

"May I ask you a personal question, if you allow me", the old man asked gently taking a sip from the freshly prepared tea from the glass.

"Yeah please! You may ask me anything", I said taking a seat on the side to face the old and a decent man.

"No one from your family has been admitted in this hospital that I am sure and also you don't work here as well".

"Yeah Right! But how do get to know this?", I was surprised to see this man guessing everything right and I was meeting him for the first time.

"People of your generation to keep looking into their phones for most of the time, and you must be doing the same, but right now you are constantly looking only at the gate and waiting for someone", he said with an added sarcasm for the generation X.

However, I was not looking to defend my generation for all the good things they are doing and explain him the generation gap which has developed and you all are equally responsible for that. So I moved the topic to myself saying,

"Yes, I have lost contact with one my dearest friend and I am waiting to get a clue as to where I could find her".

"Do you love her?", was his next question.

"No, we are just good friends, I love someone else. But she married someone else and left me alone. I was in a lot of pain and despair when I met Aditi and she took care of me from then on taking me out of all the hardships I had to go through. Tears rolled down my eyes as I started to share the things.

"Don't cry! Beta", the old man said, handing me his handkerchief. I wiped out my tears and held the object in my hand as I was sure that I will need it many more times now.

"If you are comfortable with me, can you share your story to me, I can be of some help to you I am sure", he said as he ordered tea for both of us and light up his BIDI to smoke.

"You know this is a natural product and it will harmless", he said with a laughter.

"Beta it is very easy to give suggestion to someone else, but very difficult to follow. Cigarette and tea together are injurious to health my father told me when he caught me smoking and since them I am smoking Bidi. He said and we both laughed together with a loud voice getting everybody's attention. I was habituated to this situation before also of getting attention in a crowded place so I was not worried and nobody can dare to stare the old man because people feel and get inspired looking such old age people enjoying and laughing. Our society and movies have always presented the old age people in a miserable state with a lot of pain and agony, that they get so much of sympathy from everyone except the family they belong to. However, I light up the Bidi for myself and started to narrate my story to this gentleman, right from the trip to Mumbai to the point I have reached here to sit beside him in this tea shop. The handkerchief looked like it has been soaked in water with my tears. I just got up and washed my face with the little mug of water near the tea stall and wiped out my face with my shirt as the small cotton stuff was of no use to me now and sat on the bench I was sitting before.

"Bhaiya! Ek aur chai dijiyega", (one more tea) I said to the shopkeeper who was now worried about our health because not only smoking but excess tea is also injurious to health.

"Uncle, ek natural product dena", I said to old man asking for Bidi with a smile.

———◆———

Chapter 16

Lesson of life

"Sometimes in life, your situation will keep repeating itself, until you learn your LESSON"

"I am glad to hear your story", the old man started the conversation breaking the silence we were in.

"I am happy to hear from a person who belong to this generation has so much to feel and look for when it comes to LOVE and friendship".

Otherwise, when I get to see the surrounding around and look at the newspaper and channels with so many horrible incidences of boys stabbing the girls, throwing acid on faces and many other. These incidents are not good for humanity and it tells the ignorance of the people to understand love. And when it comes to celebrities from which the generation X is mostly learning and admiring, where most of them are always in the news with their hook up and breakups is also can't be defined as love. It is just a way to keep themselves in the news. The regular hook ups and break ups happen because the person still has not found his SOULMATE.

And once you find it your search is over. You will never look for it again.

You don't search the things you already found. The statement that you fall in love is also incomplete. You fall in love to rise in life. Can you imagine what two connected souls can do together, they will generate so much of strength and power that they can break all the shackles created by humanity. All the statement looked so true to me and I could feel them. I knew how I use to face everything when I was with Aarushi.

Love is the most beautiful thing that happened to you when you met and a pause by the old man to drink water from the jug added to the anxiety. I was not able to figure it out as to why his opinion mattered to me when I knew that I loved only Aarushi and Aditi is just a friend. But anyhow he finished his procedure to quench his thirst and began again......

Love is the most beautiful thing that happened to you when you met Aarushi. A sigh of relief as I heard the name for which I was very sure. Love is all about freedom there are no boundaries to it and the reason you have gone through so much of pain and agony was just because of your ignorance. All you tried was to cage Aarushi and her love for you in the prison of marriage. The only thing that mattered to you was that she did not marry you but someone else. She must have tried to tell you the reason as to why she could not marry you, but you have caged yourself so much with the thoughts of marriage that you never listened to her.

I was surprised to hear this from the old man and incidences of her coming to my place after her engagement engulfed me, when I refused to listen to her.

"And you do not need to worry about Aditi, you will find her as she must have given a clue to someone who has been watching you since the time you both were patient and doctor till the time you were close friends. She is just testing your friendship", he said, and got up from the bench.

"It is time for me to leave as you must be having a lot work to do", he said with a smile and handed over his business card.

"Ravi Kumar Storyteller", I read it and straight away asked

"What do you mean by storyteller?". One who tells stories.

I invite you to visit canvas coffee Banglore and hear some stories when I recite them.

"You perform in Banglore, so what were you doing here on this tea stall", I asked as I was amazed to hear all these.

He kept smiling for a minute and then gently whispered in my ears "I was searching a story for my next performance". And before I could figure out everything, he said

"Give your story a good end and tell me, otherwise I will give an end to your story according to me". I will be performing in two weeks time from today and you will finish your grandmother's death leave in two weeks, so let's meet them and he disappeared in his distant Audi parked just behind the tea stall.

Chapter 17

Finding Aditi

"Finding a friend is like finding a treasure."

"After the departure of the old man, I was left with two things one was to find Aditi and the second was to confront Aarushi and that also in 14 days because I cannot give the liberty of finishing my story to the old man. My life has been given a new turn by this man and I now I have an objective to it, I began my search again to find Aditi and sat on the bench and began the brainstorming session and started to visualize all the memories and incidences since I met Aditi. Everything, Everyword, and Everyplace. What we did together, which people we met together, the books we shared but clueless. I scolded myself in between for not visiting Aditi's home, even though she insisted many times. Where the clue is, I began to wonder as to whether I should believe the old man's words or I should just go with the plan I had to meet the senior doctor. Before I could come to a conclusion I heard two people talking to each other

"Yar ye coffee mujhe pasand nahi aati, apne ko jab tak chai na mile dimag kam karta hi nahi" (I don't like coffee, my mind works best with tea). BINGO! The hospital coffee shop, it was the only place where we went on a more regular basis. I jumped out of the bench and as soon as I started to run, I heard a loud voice

"Bhaiya! Paise?", the owner of the tea shop shouted.

"Sorry, sorry", and took a 100 rupee note and handed over to him. "180 for 12 tea and 4 cigarette", he said in a sarcastic tone. I just handed over another note of 100 and said "Keep the change" and rushed to the hospital coffee shop. I went straight to the billing counter and was surprised to see him smiling and pointing his finger as soon as he saw me, to the chamber of the store owner. Without thinking for a second I went to the owner.

"Excuse me!", I said as I opened the door to the chamber and saw a big fat man sitting on the chair and wearing as many gold as possible nearly covering all his body parts.

"Yeah! Sir please tell me" he said in his timid voice which did not match his personality.

"My name is Jay, I am trying to find doctor Aditi. We both use to come here and", before I could say anything else he stopped me with his fat hand.

"Wait, wait", and he opened his drawer and took out an envelope. With my name Jay. She said that you will come and all I need is to just hand over this to you.

"Thank you, thanks a lot" I said and opened the envelope. There were two letters one of which was an address for a hospital in south Delhi. I kept the other in the pocket as I thought I could read that in the cab and fetched out my most favourite gazet and booked a cab to the hospital.

TO,

The dearest friend of mine,

I know if you are reading this then you must have gone through a lot of unnecessary pain. I know my behavior towards you was not appropriate. But as you know that I do not have many friends and it was only you that I had, I was shocked to hear about your transfer. I never wanted you to be my Facebook or wtsapp friend. I did not want to be social when it comes to network with you. I never wanted you to share the same bonding of friendship as you had with me, but once you go to a distant place, I was fearful that it might happen. You said to me that we should not ruin our chemistry by entering into a relationship and I stopped myself there only and started to accept you as a friend. And after sometime I realized that my life is complete just being your friend and so I gave up all my urge to enter into a relationship with you. But the day you shared your transferred details I was shocked, the whole world came to a standstill. I was totally in despair and could not gather my thoughts which resulted in such a behavior. But after some time I realized that transfer to a different place, could not ruin our relationship because not only me, but you must also be incomplete without my presence. And since you are reading this letter I can say that I was not wrong. Come fast I am having my lunch alone for so many days. WAITING...

I wiped out the tear and asked the reception person, "Where can I find Dr Aditi's department of mental health".

"Just behind you" she replied and I turned to see the lady in her orthodox white apron.

She just rushed and hugged me and I holded her tightly as we both began to cry in the middle of the hospital and this time again, I got everybody's attention but I did not care and allowed my tears to roll down.

"Thank you, thank you for keeping my belief", she whispered in my ears.

"He is my best friend and he is the best of the best", she shouted as we regained our normal gestures. I just kept looking at her and wondered as to whether I deserved all this...!

Chapter 18

Confronting Aarushi

"When it is time for the souls to meet there is nothing on earth that can prevent them no matter where they are located."

I was overwhelmed after meeting Aditi and so was she, there can never anything more refreshing than getting a friend again. We promised each other that we will never again get separated at any cost and it is the most precious gift that we have kept all our lives. I shared the entire event with me coming to Delhi and meeting a storyteller. She was also amazed after hearing all that because it looked unimaginable to both of us. How can a person just by listening to a story can tell the exact events. However, he did it was to the likings to both of us.

The peace on Aditi's face was very much visible to me, but my mind was still wondering as I knew that one more thing needs to be cleared out before my leaves got over. I was in a dilemma situation because I did not have an idea as to how and where should I approach Aarushi and how will Aditi react to it.

I had her contact no but not the courage to call her. A guilt of not listening to her was pinching inside me. Also, I did not have the courage to ask Aditi for help because she knew everything and won't allow me to approach her. What should I do? I said to myself. I will call her, no let me drop a text to her a voice came from inside. Yes text will be fine. I will text her I decided and started to type on the gazet which I believed was best on planet earth.

Hi, just wanted to meet you if it is ok with you. Tell me the time and place and I will come. And a pause for a second before pressing the send option. My phone beeped with an amazing tone, without holding for a second I opened to read the message. The address of a hospital with the caption anytime you can come. I told Aditi that I have an important work to finish off before I rushed to the cab that I booked.

All the memories started to flash in front of me as the driver pressed the accelerator. My heart started to beat at a much faster rate than normal. The time when I first held her hand on the beach when a minor insect had troubled her flashed, how horrified I was at that moment. Memories kept popping out of my head one after the other and kept reminding of the bondage I have experienced with her before her marriage. I needed to find out the reason for such an irrational decision of her not to marry me, when I was confirming that she loved me. Why did she do that?, was the last thought I came across before the driver stopped the car in front of a large corporate hospital gate. I paid him and rushed to the reception counter.

I need to meet Aarushi Abhishek Singh, no, no Aarushi Singh I asked the gentleman sitting at the reception counter.

"Which department she works in, he replied .

"Wait, I will call and ask her", I said to him.

By this time I have regained my strength of dialing her number. One ring and she picked up the phone, "Come to room number 207", she said before I could ask her. I did not know what to say and put the phone down.

"Which way is room number 207", I asked after filling the useless paper and grabbing the visitor's card that the man was holding for me

"Second floor and seventh room on the right hand side as you get out of the lift". "Thanks", I said and ran.

My heart was pumping blood at a great pace to provide the necessary energy to all the cells which were dying because of the anxiety I was going through. I crossed room no 205, 206 and closed door 207. Gently knocked it, "Beta aa jao" (come in) I heard a voice of a lady. I opened the door just to see an old lady somewhere around my mother's age sitting on a chair and slicing some fruits. I just joined my hand together to greet her saying

"Namaste aunty".

"She is my mom and not my in laws", I heard a voice from the bed which was hiding by the door I opened. I turned towards it and gently moved in and touched the feet of the lady.

"Sit", she said, pushing a chair closer to the bed. Moment of silence from my side as I was horrified to see the pale and weak Aarushi with a stitch on her nose and a catheter on her arms which were attached to the blood bottle hanging in the air. All the dazzle that her eyes carried was lost. She has lost her charm.

"No Kajal and make up as you like", she said as tears started to flow from what could be the most beautiful eyes anyone can ever imagine.

I could not control myself and just went on to hug her. I kept holding her and she kept crying and screaming, I was very sure that she was not hungry for food but me.

A few moments of silence from everyone as I sat on the chair back again and her mother wiped Aarushi's face with a towel. I was deep into my thoughts and so was Aarushi before her mother bought a cup of tea for me and some fruits for the dying creature.

I am very sorry Jay, I was the one who stopped Aarushi from marrying you. She said, breaking the silence of the moment.

"What? You know about us" I asked.

"I know everything but you don't know many things which I will tell you today". She said and took her seat.

Life is a great mystery and a lot of unexpected things happened to me since I met you, but I never have thought the answer which I wanted from Aarushi will be given by her mother.

Around 20 years back when Aarushi was just 4 years old, my husband was running a successful business of cotton, but his business partners betrayed him and went away with all the money. We were bankrupt. At that point of time Mr Singh, Aarushi's father in law helped us with money and effort to reestablish our business and ourselves. He not only gave money, but also kept on funding the business for next 5 years, which helped us to regain our dignity in the society. He never asked for anything in return which was very generous of him. One day while Aarushi was doing her graduation, he came to us and said that his son who has returned from London after completing his MBA has seen Aarushi and very much liked her and he wants to get married to her. We had so much to pay back to Mr Singh that we said yes without any delay but still asked them to give her permission to complete her graduation and do job because she wanted to be self dependent women. Her father explained Aarushi about the things that happened and how did Mr Singh help him to come out of it, and Now it was their responsibility to pay back. She just obliged him and said YES for the marriage. But real problem started when Abhishek started to behave as an inspector to her. He started to keep eyes on all her stuff. Still, my daughter was avoiding all the things and I also pushed her not to break the relation as it was not only about both of you but the entire family. She never uttered a word and kept her silence until she met you.... And everything after that, you know. She never wanted to marry him, but her father forced her and I begged her to do so.

"I am very sorry beta", she said, and started to cry.

I took some time to recollect all that has been said and moved to Aarushi to kiss her forehead and said "Bye, hope we meet again".

"We will", she replied and handed me a letter which was below her pillow. It looked more or less like Aarushi, the paper has lost its strength and charm,it must have been written decades ago but still it had many things to say. I took it, kept it in my pocket and left.

———— ◆ ————

Chapter 19

Canvas café

"Close your eyes and hear the silence for silence has much more to say than words. All these years I was dying to hear from her without understanding that she was speaking through her silence."

"I always wanted to confront you with the reason as to why I cannot marry you but never got enough courage. I can never forget the day when you became the part of my life. You did not look like a stranger to me.

You touched the most fragile parts of my heart and soul and made them yours.

I know that I will never meet anyone who would love me as you did.

I know that I will never meet anyone who would take care of me as you did.

I will never be able to forget the way you keep staring at me all day and all night long. I felt like the heavens in your arm,

The way you begged me not to put Kajal in eyes as I looked better without them.

The way you massaged me when I used to come after work, the way you maintained the first aid box for me in case I got an asthma attack. Everything you did was happening to me for the first time, although I have been in a relation since long. I thank you for caring for me so much, still I hurted you a lot and lied to you many times, and I am really very sorry for it. I hurted you because I never wanted to lie to you and lied to you because I did not want to hurt you. Because of me, you have to go through a lot of pain and I plead you to forgive me.

With all the great things that I felt since I met you, I have few questions to ask you,

Have you ever imagined a situation, what I felt when I had to sit and perform rituals of marriage with a person whom I do not love. Tell me what should I answer a person who ask me that it is his right to have to sex with me since I am married to him. Imagine a situation when your body is played with just in the name of love making against your will. Imagine what I must have felt while keeping a fast for a person for his long life, who do not care to take me to a doctor when I was suffering from illness.

All this happens with me every day and I face them along with just only one hope that you will understand me someday, although the day might come after a lifetime, in our next birth...

We were meant to be together because we complete each other beautifully in every possible sense and our love will last for many lifetimes to come.

"I will wait for you
I will die for you
and
I will find you
because
I love you"

Thank you, said the storyteller with these lines. Nobody clapped, No one applauded, but a SILENCE…!

———————◆———————

Chapter 20

The journey continued

"Life is a journey, so is love."

"I Letting go of a deeply embedded relationship after pouring years of heart, mind and soul is not an easy task. The person can go through a unique series of thoughts and emotions. But once you have the hope of meeting again all the emotions of despair and darkness just vanishes and you start to live.

Two years have passed since I have met Aarushi in the hospital. I never called her, neither did she. I never followed her on social media neither did she. All my questions were answered. I am not sad anymore, I am not disoriented anymore.

I continued to grow my life exponentially, I started my own business. I wanted to fulfill all the expectation that my pears had with me. My friendship with Aditi continued to flourish, adding strength. I never told her about Aarushi neither did she ever asked.

I understood that we never lose people whom we love, they continue to accompany us in every act, thought and decision making. Their love has left an imprint on our memories which empowers us at every point of time. We find comfort even in their absence.

I have overcome the fear of losing people, I have overcome pain. I have overcome the fear of failure. I have overcome the biggest fear of mankind DEATH because I know that WE WILL MEET AGAIN....

……….. I know that we have met before and I know that we will meet again. I will find my way to you in the next life and every life after that. MIA HOLLOW.

About the Author

A simple and fun loving boy Jayant Bhagat is the co-founder of Athanasius a pharma company.

He has worked as a sales executive and manager in top companies like Novartis and SRL Diagnostic after completing his graduation in Bachelors of pharmacy.

"Then I Met You" is his debut novel and he is planning to write in many other niche of the society which touches the hearts of the reader and inspires them at the same time.